Goodnight, Sadi Moose

a bedtime story by
Dana Pegram

ilustrated by
Doina Paraschiv

Copyright © 2019 by Dana Pegram
All rights reserved. This book or any portion thereof
may not be reproduced or used in any manner whatsoever
without the express written permission of the publisher
except for the use of brief quotations in a book review.

This book is a work of fiction. Names, characters, places and incidents are either the product of the author's imagination or are used fictitiously, and any resemblance to actual persons, living or dead, business establishments, events, or locales is entirely coincidental.

Printed in the United States of America

First Printing, 2019

ISBN/SKU:9780578578361
ISBN Complete:978-0-578-57836-1

www.DanaPegram.com

Dedication

To my great niece and nephew, Jordyn and Jalen who's boundless energy gives me great joy.

When the sun begins to set and darkness fills the sky

Sadi shuffles to her bed and waits for Mommy and Daddy to tuck her in.

Sadi Moose is ready to sleep but won't close her eyes until Daddy reads her a story and Mommy sings a lullaby.

Today she's had lots and lots of fun

splashing in rain puddles and running through the woods loose.

She's had a bubbly bubble bath

Mommy and Daddy's footsteps can be heard down the hall and a soft, angelic sound of Mommy humming a sweet, sweet song.

Sadi finally closes her eyes.

As the sky dims its lights
Mommy tucks her tightly
they both kiss her on the cheek
and wish her goodnight.

Coloring Pages

Activity Pages

Say What You See

I	Me	You
It	He	She
We	Go	To

Add Me Up

© Dana Pegram 2019

From the Author:

As a young girl I found inspiration for writing through the lens of a world I wanted to create. I started out writing Poetry, Short Stories and Screenplays before penning my first children's book. As a teacher, I have become more passionate about creating stories for young children that will allow them to fall in love with reading.